SASHA

Tears of Regret

Stolen Moments

ASA PUBLISHING CORPORATION
AN INNOVATIVE OUTSOURCE BOOK PUBLISHING HYBRID

1285 N. Telegraph Rd., #376, Monroe, Michigan 48162
An Accredited Publishing House with the BBB
www.asapublishingcorporation.com

Copyrights©2020, Steven Lawrence Hill Sr., All Rights Reserved
Book Title: SASHA *Tears of Regret: Stolen Moments*
Date Published: 03.20.2020
Book ID: ASAPCID2380803
Edition: 1 *Trade Paperback*
ISBN: 978-1-946746-73-3
Library of Congress Cataloging-in-Publication Data

This book was published in the United States of America.
Great State of Michigan

INTRODUCTION

Sasha is a mixed Puerto Rican and white Philadelphian girl from a blue-collar, working-class family. She works part-time at a Walmart Supercenter on Christopher Columbus Boulevard during her high school years up to graduation day and then was given an opportunity for a full-time position soon afterward. Eight months down the road, Sasha becomes an assistant manager, progressing her employment into a steady working career. Two years after that, she meets this fair-looking young mulatto man wearing faded jeans and a hoodie named Daniel in her store trying to exchange some meat products because he was given the wrong produce by accident, but later it was straightened out. A year had passed, she marries him, and a few months then after, she becomes pregnant.

Things are going great, Sasha has her own nucleus family and moved into her own home a few blocks away from her parents, and now lives on Bonsall Street, only 18 minutes away from her job. She had been promoted to a manager, her husband got a job as a road worker for the City of Philadelphia, and now they have a son, Benjamin.

PRELUDE

With children growing up so fast these days, it's hard to believe that little Benjamin is now three years old today on this beautiful Saturday afternoon. Sasha is coming in the house from Walmart with her son's birthday cake in her hand, her husband Daniel blowing up balloons and sticking them on the walls while guests are slowly pouring in for the little one's birthday party. Yes, June 29th, 2019, a milestone for Benjamin with a few supporting family members and some neighborhood friends with their children coming together to create a small celebration for him.

"Hey honey, is Benjamin's grandparents coming over for the birthday party?"

"No, I just got off the phone with them. Both of my parents will be working late."

"Wow Hun, they're always working . . . it's Saturday for Christ's sake!" responding while having a balloon partially hanging out of his mouth.

"Do me a favor and go check the AC in the other room? Thanks. The thermometer outside the doorway said that it's about 91 degrees when I was coming in."

"No problem, got you covered." Daniel grunts in humor as he releases his pinch from another balloon that he was working on spurted out across the room with that screechy air noise.

Sasha looks at her husband and smiles, "Boys will be boys," then hugs her son and scoots him over to play with the rest of the kids while she goes and asks for some volunteers to take Daniel's place with the balloons.

She was never really worried about the grandparents on both sides, not showing up. In fact, it didn't matter much to her because she knew that her parents worked a lot, and she never met Daniel's parents; he never talks about them, only about his big brother Darion who showed up to the party. Darion was one of those well-dress preppy-like Versace looking gentleman with circle specs glasses who has a very high expensive taste.

But as for the birthday party itself, it continued moving right along, a beautiful snapshot Kodak moment in time. There were pictures being taken with their cell phones, music playing in the background, balloons being smacked and kicked around by some of the children. Others singing happy birthday while Sasha holding up to the table a 12" x 18" Vanilla Sheet Cake with whipped Buttercream icing, and a huge lit candle designed like the number #3 in the center. It was the typical setting in the afternoon for a child's beautiful birthday party on South Bonsall Street in Philadelphia, Pennsylvania. Peaceful.

Then it happened, the humidity began taking its course. Guests were starting to feel their clothes becoming a bit sticky with the moisture in the air. Some started talking amongst themselves about how the heat is making them become a little sweaty. A few adults with open beer bottles clanging them together in agreement that maybe it's time to call it an evening.

Sasha walks over to her husband. "Babe, I thought that you checked the AC?"

"I did. Everything appeared to be working fine. There's only one notch left, and that's max."

"Do something! Everyone is getting a little fidgety because of the heat."

"Okay – okay, I got this!" Daniel looks around the room, locating where everyone is assembling on the second floor of their house, trying to see if anyone is going to listening to him. "Hold up everyone, . . . Can I have your attention, please?"

While he is waiting for everyone to get themselves together, Sasha is walking over to their stereo system and lowering down the music a bit, giving her husband a couple of nods in a gesture to go ahead and speak.

"Good. No need to hurry out, there's more cake for the kids, more beer (everyone chuckles), so hang tight while I turn up the AC in the other room."

"You are going to leave the door open this time, aren't you?" someone blurts out while getting a couple of giggles in from a few other guests.

"Yeah – yeah!" As he sits his piece of cake on the table, picks up a beer and waving his hand while holding it as he exits down into the hallway.

In the meantime, this well-dressed man with glasses, Darion, walks over to the front windows, and open's one of them halfway. It was mid-summer, and inside was continually getting very humid, even though there was an air conditioning unit already on in one of the windows in the next room down the hallway. He then walked away to get some more fruit punch.

"Hey, aren't you Darion, my husband's older brother?" Trying to catch him before he finished walking back across the room. Darion wasn't a social drinker.

"Sure," while grabbing himself a cup of fruit punch.

"What kind of answer is that?" Shrugging her shoulders. Anyway, can you close the window, there's no screen in it, and my husband will be back in a few moments."

Darion nods then fade off into a non-seeable distance

with his drink.

Meanwhile, the young father is at the air conditioner in the other room, baffled as to why it is off, and the turn-on knob is missing. "Wow, that's odd. I gotta go get some vise grips to get this thing back in motion."

But unfortunately, no sooner than later, the little birthday boy saw this shiny red balloon caught in a slight air vacuum coming from the window, and it's squeezing its way partially out onto the open-air now stuck between the window and the frame. The little boy, Benjamin, somehow escapes the attention of everyone, gets up from the table and chases after the balloon. Once he touched it, the balloon got sucked in the air. Its string caught onto a tree branch two and a half stories up, a few feet within a distance of the window. The child begins to climb onto the ledge to go after it. The mother, Sasha, calling out her son's name because he wasn't sitting where she left him. Everyone appeared as though they were in a time-bubble the way Sasha plowed herself through them to get to her son.

As her husband finally comes back in to let her know why it took him so long, he lifts his head, followed her eyes, and dropped his now empty beer bottle crashing on the floor, as she is still pushing her guests out the way.

Her husband yells out, "Sasha!"

They both looking over at the window where their precious son is almost entirely over the edge. Both are racing around the table to get to him. Sasha being closer, grabbed his tiny little fingers on one of his hands just in time, but misfortune has taken its toll. The little boy looks at his mother one last time, smiling - pointing at the balloon and pushing himself off the outside wall saying, "Mommy, balloon!" Benjamin's mother tries to calm the little one down telling him to stop rocking back and forth, and her husband continually yelling at her, "Don't you dare let him go . . . Don't you let him go, ya' hear me!!!"

Both parents in a panic and dire desperation to stop the inevitable, his tiny little fingers slip right through Sasha's grip. Screaming in spurts of pain as Benjamin's body topples on tree limbs after tree limbs, pretzeling his small little body - head first bashing itself against the pavement where there were other children out on the sidewalk playing. Now screaming in horror as the blood of a three-year-old splash across their clothing; Sasha being traumatized watching little Benjamin the whole way down until the branches with trickles of blood on them returned to its form, restricting visual, except the screams from below. Others were running out of their homes in witness of little Benjamin's fate while this shiny red balloon floats into the clouds, never again to return.

SASHA

SASHA

Tears of Regret

Stolen Moments

STEVEN LAWRENCE HILL SR

CHAPTER ONE

The Family Nucleus

June 29th, 2024, five years had passed where there used to be a house on the corner of South Bonsall and Oakford St., where a couple used to live, even after the death of their three-year-old son; a family nucleus ripped apart into darkness. Only hollow whispers remain in the streets of South Philadelphia's backdrops of what went on in there. The two and a half story tree where the little red balloon hung in is still there to this day, now over towering the rest of the homes in the neighborhood.

Some of the new children in Landreth School often spoke about the other kids before them telling stories of old fables of a little boy running down the nursery hallways with his small red balloon, just a few blocks away.

Grown folks were mentioning to each other about the abduction of a young woman in the home who became known as a heroin addict, how her husband used to have this barricade, gate-type doors going into the vestibule. Sasha's parents were getting unknown calls in the middle of the night, no-one answering, just a squeaky voice, and heavy breathing.

With tears of regret looking at this empty corner lot where her home once stood, now only vines crawling across the walls of other houses, bushes filling up spaces, and that damn tree helping Sasha remember this all too well.

As Sasha got back into the taxi, she still could not accept why her son had to die as he did because of what her husband had put her through. She now knows it wasn't a coincidence, as she carries the burden of a hefty price that contributed to little Benjamin's death.

"Ma'am, where would you like to go next?"

Tears still trickling. "Drive, . . . just drive – anywhere, I don't care. This has been another stolen moment for me."

"Ma'am? . . ." Before he could say another word, Sasha looked up at him through the mirror with this stare that only another victim would understand. The taxi driver put his vehicle in gear and continued heading southbound to the other end of the corner of Bonsall St. facing the park in front, then made a left.

After about 15 minutes driving down the road, Sasha begins opening her purse, counting mixed bills.

"Driver, do me a favor and stop by Russell's Pawn Shop, I would like to pick up something along the way."

Looking through his rearview mirror, the taxi driver sees Sasha fumbling through a whole wad of cash. With apparent confidence in having a paying customer, he radios in to the station informing dispatch to hold his calls.

Taxi Driver: By-the-way, what's the best route to Russell's Pawn Shop from my location?

Dispatch: Turn right on Pine, then make a left on 9th Street. As soon as you get past Starbucks, you should be right there.

Taxi Driver: Copy.

The taxi driver then turns his direction to the customer, arm leaning on top of the seat against the plexiglass.

"Ma'am, we're about only 3 minutes out."

"Doesn't matter, just let me know when we arrive," responded Sasha. "When we get there, keep it running, I'm not going to be that long."

"Yes, ma'am."

"Please," looking up towards the front with shrewd arrogance, "call me SASHA. You don't know me well enough." Then taps the plexiglass with a fist full of cash, the taxicab driver pushes down the lift, she drops the money in, he closes it takes the money out, stops the vehicle, then places it in park.

"We're here."

Sasha then gets out, goes into the Pawn Shop walks up to the counter.

"You got what I was looking for?"

The clerk reaches under the counter, pulls out a triangle leather pouch, and two boxes of hollow points. Then placed both hands on the glass counter, each outside of the pouch. Sasha spins the zipper side around to her and opens it. She looked up at the clerk sits her medium size purse on top of the glass counter, pulls out two rolls, picks up this man-handler, and stuffs it in her purse, then precede to casually walk back out, like a woman on a mission. It was an American Classic 1911 Commander handgun; a silver 45 ACP (Automatic Colt Pistol) single action with center-bored hollow-point bullets to go, diamond-cut wooden grip single clip with a 4.3 barrel, which holds eight rounds. And it has a nice weight of about 2.3 lbs.

She gets back in the taxi, sits her purse on her lap, eyes looking at the street names on the corner through the back right-side taxi door window, then tapping the outside center of her purse.

"I'm good, . . . that seafood joint on North Broad Street."

The driver looking forward without question puts the vehicle in drive and back out onto the road again, hitting his turn signal. Sasha had a feeling, knowing her husband Daniel, he could not resist staying in Philadelphia, let alone be at one of his private hangout spots. She figures it's time for him to pay the devil's due – Benjamin's soul comes calling, and someone's gotta answer for it.

A twenty-three-minute ride to a seafood restaurant to see if her husband is still that naïve seems like a lifetime for Sasha. Awake and subconsciously drifting into each moment that brought her to this place in time. Unanswered questions that grind her heart, a wedding that should have never taken place . . . how much was I worth? Well, a hollow-point to the kneecap should be an excellent start.

As the taxicab driver drives up and pulls in, Sasha could see Daniel's head sticking out from one of the booths with what looks like a piece of crab leg sticking out of his mouth.

"That stupid-stupid son-of-a-bitch! I knew it, . . . just couldn't take his high-yellow ass out of Philadelphia, now could he?!" in complete anger, putting her purse back over her shoulder. "Well, I got somethin' for that ass!"

The driver knowing that Sasha is about to do something that he'll regret staying for, let's her out at the front entrance then drives away. Sasha looking at him pulling out, hawks one up and spits hard onto the ground. No respect needed, and she could care less what the taxicab driver was thinking. She wasn't here to eat lobster tails. No, it was about cracking that dome on her husband's head. But first, she needs answers.

As Sasha walked in, she was met by the restaurant's greeter, "Good afternoon and welcome to *The Reef*," while opening her reservation folder. "Do you have a reserve . . ."

"No, but I am here meeting someone," interrupted Sasha, tapping on the side of her purse again.

"Oh, well you can wait over there and . . ."

Sasha, irritated on the suspense, helped the greeter put her open reservation folder down on the greet podium by gently pushing on the greeter's hand softly then rolled her eyes with this Chessy Cat grin, pointing with the other.

"No need to wait, my HUSBAND is right over there, adjacent to the bar."

"Where?"

"Look again, Hun." Directing her eyes to a specific booth. "The one who can't stop smacking those lips together with all that fish in his mouth."

The greeter looked at her like she couldn't wait to get off this shift. Sasha's whole demeanor was making the greeter a little nervous.

"Auh, uh-huh, . . . sure. Right this way, follow me, ma'am."

"Please don't call me that."

The greeter struggled to put on a fake smile, but somehow she managed without saying a word and escorted her to the booth where Sasha's husband is sitting and still eating.

Daniel looked up in shock, dropping pieces of seafood out of his mouth.

"Oh, don't get up on my account. I'm no lady today, . . . there, sit back down."

The greeter looking at both of them, all she could think right now is, 'Lord, please don't let this be a cat and dog fight before my shift is over. I still need a little more tips so I can pay my electric bill tomorrow morning.'

"Well, may I get you a menu and perhaps something to drink?"

"You know what, as a matter of fact, bring me some breadsticks and a bottle of Merlo if you got any," retorted Sasha.

"Breadsticks?" her husband questioned.

"Yea, nigga, just how you like feeding your ho's after you've snatched them up."

The greeter muffled her cough as if she was choking for just a brief interruption. "Very good, I'll go get that wine for you," scuttling away, trying not to get pulled into that scene.

As she leaves, Sasha stares at her husband in a very dark

way, sits the purse on the seat of the booth, unzips it, pulls out the .45, and taps it under the table. Daniel, hearing it repetitiously – one tap after another looks at her with this curious look, picks up a napkin and begins wiping his mouth.

Sasha, being infuriated with his *womanizing demeanor* actions, smirked at him and said in a shallow and angry tone, "You lowdown dirty no good mother fuckin' bitch of a husband, you want this or not?!" Then taps under the table again a couple more times, this time with her finger on the trigger.

Daniel scoots a little to the side to look under the table, and when he does . . .

"Don't you dare put your hands on it!"

As soon as Daniel immediately sits back up, Sasha had already grabbed a handful of seafood off his plate and then flicked it at him.

"What the Fu . . . ?"

"I'm not gonna ask you this again, now do you want it?! A simple yes or no will do?"

You can see it in the pupils of Daniel's eyes that everything which has been done to poor Sasha for all those years had come back to haunt him. It was like looking in a mirror. All Sasha needed now is to hear echos of happy birthday songs in the air from anyone to put that index trigger finger in motion.

It seems like almost just in time, after going out back to take a smoke break from all the craziness, the greeter tries to regroup herself, comes back in and looks through the port of one of the swinging doors to see if they're still at it. Knowing that she doesn't want to lose her job over a customer's relationship dispute puts on a happy face, and brings out the small order anyway. The timing couldn't be more perfect, at least for the moment.

"Here you go, your breadsticks and wine. If you need anything else, our waiter assigned to this booth (looking at Daniel and then back to Sasha) will continue to serve you."

Daniel looks like a mess, Sasha grabbing a breadstick and chomping on it in such a trifling way, yet both of them are now having a tough time looking away from each other in fear what the other might do next.

"Well, my name is Katie, it was a pleasure, and again, welcome to *The Reef*," then took long and fast strides from the booth.

"You got a lot of balls coming in here acting a fool, Sasha!" Daniel brushing himself off.

"And you don't?" Sasha's eyes were getting a little watery, her hand shaking and getting sweaty under the table, that American Classic 1911 which are chambered in with hollow-points wanting to be called to action.

For a few moments, there was complete and total silence. People in other booths, bars, and tables were still carrying on with their meals, but as for Daniel and Sasha, it was that brief few minutes of quietness to absorb horrifying flashbacks while staring into each other's eyes.

"I'll tell you what, . . . tell that to Benjamin if God gives you a chance to see him!"

Tears are turning into a rage as she yanks the handgun out from under the table, finger still on the trigger, and whisks it right in front of her husband's face.

"But, wait-wait-wait-wait . . . wait!" Daniel turned his head sideways, squinting his eyes and placing his hands over his face, covering part of his ears in fear."

Trigger pulled, "BLLLOUW!"

A hollow-point leaving the chamber dismembering almost half of the head, leaving brain matter, hair, and skull fragments everywhere. You can hear the screams of customers trampling over themselves, trying to get out of the restaurant. No rest for the Angel of Death. A pierced soul now is taken to call and another in debt of forgiveness, as one left in tears calling out to God asking why, and the other dripping all over the table in blood, motionless.

I hope you enjoyed the Sneak Peek

Preview of

"SASHA"

Vol 1 of 3

If you would like to know when the book is

released just go to or press here:

https://www.asapublishingcorporation

.com/steven-hill

and subscribe.

SASHA Vol 1

SASHA Vol 1

SASHA Vol 1

SASHA Vol 1

SASHA Vol 1

SASHA Vol 1

SASHA Vol 1

SASHA Vol 1

SASHA Vol 1

SASHA Vol 1

SASHA Vol 1

SASHA Vol 1

SASHA Vol 1

SASHA Vol 1

SASHA Vol 1

SASHA Vol 1

SASHA Vol 1

SASHA Vol 1

SASHA Vol 1

SASHA Vol 1

SASHA Vol 1

SASHA Vol 1

SASHA Vol 1

SASHA Vol 1

SASHA Vol 1

SASHA Vol 1

SASHA Vol 1

SASHA Vol 1

SASHA Vol 1

SASHA Vol 1

SASHA Vol 1

SASHA Vol 1

SASHA Vol 1

SASHA Vol 1

SASHA Vol 1

SASHA Vol 1

SASHA Vol 1

SASHA Vol 1

SASHA Vol 1

SASHA Vol 1

SASHA Vol 1

SASHA Vol 1

SASHA Vol 1

SASHA Vol 1

SASHA Vol 1

SASHA Vol 1

SASHA Vol 1

SASHA Vol 1

SASHA Vol 1

SASHA Vol 1

SASHA Vol 1

SASHA Vol 1

SASHA Vol 1

SASHA Vol 1

SASHA Vol 1

SASHA Vol 1

SASHA Vol 1

SASHA Vol 1

SASHA Vol 1

SASHA Vol 1

SASHA Vol 1

SASHA Vol 1

SASHA Vol 1

SASHA Vol 1

SASHA Vol 1

SASHA Vol 1

SASHA Vol 1

SASHA Vol 1

SASHA Vol 1

SASHA Vol 1

SASHA Vol 1

SASHA Vol 1

SASHA Vol 1

SASHA Vol 1

SASHA Vol 1

SASHA Vol 1

SASHA Vol 1

SASHA Vol 1

SASHA Vol 1

SASHA Vol 1

SASHA Vol 1

SASHA Vol 1

SASHA Vol 1

SASHA Vol 1

SASHA Vol 1

SASHA Vol 1

SASHA Vol 1

SASHA Vol 1

SASHA Vol 1

SASHA Vol 1

SASHA Vol 1

SASHA Vol 1

SASHA Vol 1

SASHA Vol 1

SASHA Vol 1

SASHA Vol 1

SASHA Vol 1

SASHA Vol 1

SASHA Vol 1

SASHA Vol 1

SASHA Vol 1

SASHA Vol 1

SASHA Vol 1

SASHA Vol 1

SASHA Vol 1

SASHA Vol 1

SASHA Vol 1

SASHA Vol 1

SASHA Vol 1

SASHA Vol 1

SASHA Vol 1

SASHA Vol 1

SASHA Vol 1

SASHA Vol 1

SASHA Vol 1

SASHA Vol 1

SASHA Vol 1

SASHA Vol 1

SASHA Vol 1

SASHA Vol 1

SASHA Vol 1

SASHA Vol 1

SASHA Vol 1

SASHA Vol 1

SASHA Vol 1

SASHA Vol 1

SASHA Vol 1

SASHA Vol 1

SASHA Vol 1

SASHA Vol 1

SASHA Vol 1

SASHA Vol 1

SASHA Vol 1

SASHA Vol 1

SASHA Vol 1

SASHA Vol 1

SASHA Vol 1

SASHA Vol 1

SASHA Vol 1

SASHA Vol 1

SASHA Vol 1

SASHA Vol 1

SASHA Vol 1

SASHA Vol 1

SASHA Vol 1

SASHA Vol 1

SASHA Vol 1

SASHA Vol 1

SASHA Vol 1

SASHA Vol 1

SASHA Vol 1

SASHA Vol 1

SASHA Vol 1

SASHA Vol 1

SASHA Vol 1

SASHA Vol 1

SASHA Vol 1

SASHA Vol 1

SASHA Vol 1

SASHA Vol 1

SASHA Vol 1

SASHA Vol 1

SASHA Vol 1

SASHA Vol 1

SASHA Vol 1

SASHA Vol 1

SASHA Vol 1

SASHA Vol 1

SASHA Vol 1

SASHA Vol 1

SASHA Vol 1

SASHA Vol 1

SASHA Vol 1

SASHA Vol 1

SASHA Vol 1

SASHA Vol 1

www.ingramcontent.com/pod-product-compliance
Lightning Source LLC
Chambersburg PA
CBHW022152240626
47153CB00007B/2623